Driver and Other Stories

Femdom Mind Control

Flash Fiction – Vol. 43

S.B.

Disclaimer

This is a work of fiction. Names, characters, business, events, and incidents are the products of the author's imagination. Any resemblance to actual persons, living or dead, or actual events is purely coincidental. All characters are over 18.

Table of Contents

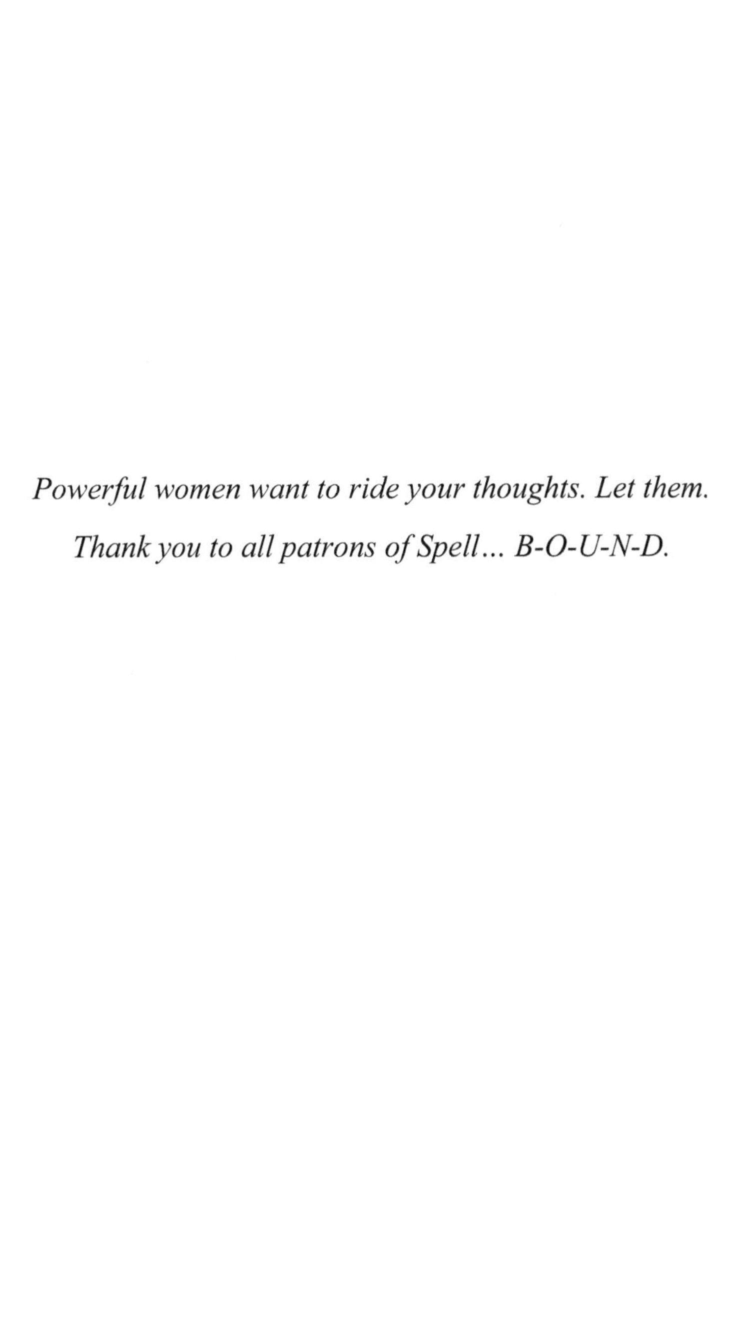

Powerful women want to ride your thoughts. Let them.

Thank you to all patrons of Spell... B-O-U-N-D.

Day Off

Emma yawned and looked at the digital clock atop her nightstand. It was half-past nine in the morning, the weekend had finally arrived and, for the first time since the beginning of the month, she felt calm and relaxed, nothing weighing on her mind.

"Hmmm, the joy of a couple of days to myself..." she mumbled, resting her arms to the side of her petite body. A fluffy Norwegian Forest cat rested on the pillow next to her, golden eyes fixed on the subtle movements of her fingers. Ratchet was a free spirit, unperturbed by anything except the lack of food. Licking his front right paw, it was almost as if he was saying, "Sure, Emma, but don't forget the tuna."

Emma stretched and tried to get up, the muscles in her body demanding yet a few more minutes before kicking into gear. It had been a restless night with her neighbor's birthday party going strong until the first light of the day. Understandable yet still a drag. Hopefully, her nineteenth anniversary wouldn't turn out to be so obnoxious.

She continued to lay quietly, musing on what to do with her time. The first order of business was to get some groceries for the week including a new bag of cat food, of course, but then what? Cleaning up her wardrobe could wait until her vacation and there was no way she was ironing with one hundred and five degrees outside. Perhaps she could finally stream the last season of her favorite sci-fi show. Weren't critics saying it was the best of them all?

"Oh, I think you have something far more important to take care of, don't you?" she heard a soft voice playing in her head like a siren's song.

"No, I don't think that's..." her train of thought was suddenly interrupted by the orgasmic flow coursing through her tight pussy. Vaginal fluids dripped down her legs leaving a warm puddle on the pink linen sheets. Ratchet perked his ears and circled her to see what the fuss was all about. "Oh, my God!"

"Goddess," the sensual voice corrected her. "Go take care of yourself first but then your time is all mine. Obey."

"Yes," Emma rose from the bed, ecstatic yet embarrassed. It had happened again, just like she had been told she would. Laziness was for the weak, not mind-controlled toys. Goddess' triggers were always waiting in the back of her head for the right moment to strike and she had no choice but to obey.

Emma cleaned herself and drove quickly to the supermarket, all the while hoping that the memories of her subconscious wouldn't play another trick on her. She left as quickly as she walked inside, with three paper bags full of everything she needed and more. The brown leather collar was the outlier, and she didn't even remember taking it to the register.

Back home, she emptied the bags and made sure Ratchet had plenty of food and water before dashing away to her hypnotic owner's place, halfway across town. The collar was already around her neck when the older blonde Amazon answered the door, holding in her hands the rest of her outfit for the day.

"Right on time," the mesmerizing woman said. Emma's conditioning had never failed her before and would be even stronger before the end of the day. Emma dropped to her knees to kiss her thigh-high leather boots and basked in her servile condition. "Hmmm, the joy of having no free will..." she mused.

Driver

Harold shivered inside the black van parked a few blocks away from Ellen Whitaker's mansion. He had a bad feeling about that night, unlike his three companions.

"Are we really going forward with this?" he asked, twiddling his thumbs.

"Of course, we are," Damian replied. He was the self-proclaimed leader of the group, and the reason they were all gathered. "Why are you so worried?"

"It's just that we never tried anything like this before. Are we sure we can pull off this heist?"

"Would I have brought you here if I wasn't? I've gone through the plan a thousand times already and there's no way this doesn't work. Are you guys having the same doubts as him?" Damian turned to the other two men.

"No, we're with you," Frank and Brian replied in unison. They were twins, with Frank being the older of two by six minutes, but their thought patterns were always perfectly synchronized. Damian had always come through for them in the past, so why would things be any different now?

"Good. Listen, Harold. This will be a cakewalk. They disable the alarms outside, I go in and get the goods and you drive us out of here. In ten minutes, we'll be filthy rich and won't have to worry about a thing for the rest of our lives."

"Unless we get caught by the police... or worse."

"Worse?" Damian scoffed. "Come on! You don't really believe Ellen Whitaker is a witch, do you? And even if the rumors were true - they're not, because witches aren't real! - she's not going to magically teleport back here to turn us into frogs or something! Get real, will you?"

"I hope you're right," Harold grumbled, hands behind the wheel. "Tell me when you're ready to go because the sooner I'm out of here the better."

"Brian? Frank? Are you good?"

"Let's do this," the brothers said.

Harold watched in dismay as his three friends exited the van. They were making a mistake. No matter what Damian believed in his aggrandizing mind, they were petty thieves at best. Stealing a car or two? No problem but going for the high-security abode of one of the most famous socialites in the city was simply too much. He tried to remain calm as he smoked a cigarette, already anticipating his next move. If they didn't make it back in fifteen minutes tops, they would be left behind to fend for themselves.

"You'd really do that to your companions?" a sinister voice purred in the passenger's seat. "That's not very nice, isn't it?"

"What the...?" he dropped the cigarette on his lap as he glimpsed the translucent dark-haired beauty sitting next to him. Emily Whitaker was there, yet she wasn't, scheming icy eyes staring him down like a huntress who had just found her prey.

"Shhh, relax... I'm not going to hurt you. You're just the driver, right? You would never dare to enter my house and ransack my property, or would you?"

"Please don't turn me into anything unnatural," Harold mumbled as a ghostly hand reached for his disheveled hair.

"Awww, I would never do that, Mr. Driver, but I think it's time you let me take the wheel."

Harold's eyes went blank as she touched his forehead.

* * *

Thirteen minutes and twenty-two seconds later, Damian and the twins returned to the van. Against all odds, their break-in had been a successful one, and the leader of the pack had kept his word. The two necklaces he had stolen - one with over fifty rubies and the other with a diamond as big as a golf ball were more than enough for a permanent vacation once they were sold in the black market. Success was assured.

"Jackpot! What did I tell you, Harold?" Damian chuckled. "You were worried about nothing. Let's roll."

Harold looked somberly at him, malice burning behind his darkened eyes.

"Yes, let's... this will be a ride you'll never forget."

The possessed puppet hit the gas, and the van drove off into the cold night. It's been missing ever since.

Final Question

It was the most surprising night ever at the old Star Auditorium. For the first time in over twelve years, a participant in the long-running contest "Who Are You?" had made it to the final round with the chance to win the prize millions of ensnared souls coveted but dared not verbalize: his freedom.

His name was Benjamin Wallace, known to the system only as Slave 420624, a lowly worker from the copper mines who had been selected alongside fifty of his peers to entertain the Free Folk over the course of six hours of peak television. The contest had it all, from displays of physical strength to random trivia few people alive could answer, and even an improv Battle Royale sequence where the primary goal was to maim as many opponents as possible suffering no long-lasting injuries oneself. It was chaotic, brutal, and a ratings favorite especially when things went south. It was also supposed to be unbeatable.

Despite no official confirmation by the producers or any of the New Amazonian Movement's Council members, everyone knew what happened backstage. All who were selected to play on the show were drugged before the cameras started shooting, their mental capabilities dulled as much as possible while still allowing them to operate on a semi-autonomous level. One way or another, they had to succumb to the challenges presented before them, usually in the most dramatic ways possible. If anyone were to defy such expectations, heads were sure to roll.

Samantha Taylor had been with the competition since its debut, hosting the weekly events with the same fake smiles and colorful clothes. She always knew what to say to keep the audience engaged and yet she too was taken aback by Benjamin's resilience in face of tremendous adversity. A right answer to the last question of the night was all that separated him from a new life beyond the menial programming installed in his mind.

"Oh wow," she said, sweat dripping down her Botox-filled forehead. "How exciting is this, everyone? 420624, do you realize what's at stake here should you answer this next question correctly?"

"Yes," Benjamin replied, spitting blood at her varnished designer shoes. The mid-thirties worker was covered in mud and small lacerations on his hands and feet, feverish eyes struggling to keep open. The roaring crowd all around was shouting his number as if it were something divine and he could get used to it. He looked at the host and said, "I'm ready for everything."

"Good. In that case, please direct your gaze to the screen behind me, for that's where your question will appear. The moment it flashes, you'll have thirty seconds to give me the right answer. Doing so will release you from the mines forever but if you fail..."

Benjamin nodded. He was already half-dead anyway so nothing could be worse than that. Reveling in the people's uncontrolled enthusiasm, he confronted the gigantic screen as it pulsated in a rapid sequence of red, white, and blue. The question was only visible for a split second before fading into nothingness.

"And there you have it, 420624. You have thirty seconds from now to give us the answer. Come on, don't keep your audience waiting," Samantha said.

"Wait, I couldn't read it..." he panicked.

"What's that?"

"The question! It flashed too quickly. I don't know what it is."

"Well, that's a shame, isn't it? I'm still going to need an answer, though. Only twenty seconds now."

"But that's not fair! You're cheating!"

"The New Amazonian Movement never cheats, 420064. It's not our fault you have a small brain, is it? Ten seconds."

"No! This is wrong," he screamed. "You can't do this! YOU CAN'T DO THIS!"

"Five, four, three, two, one... time's up!" Samantha frowned. "What a shame! So close and yet so far away. How does it feel to lose your only chance at freedom, 420624? No, don't answer that. We understand how taxing this is for you, which is why your memory will be wiped clean before you return to the mines. Guards, please escort our contestant off the stage!"

Benjamin screamed as he was being dragged away, the fickle audience now cheering for his demise. The invisible question could be only one, and the answer was as clear as day.

"Who are you?" the screen had asked. A slave and nothing more than that.

Hers

The three naked men stood before Mistress Georgia, patiently awaiting her final decision. Their names were Jonathan, Christopher, and Alec, but in her presence, they were known as 004, 012, and 023, the last remaining survivors of a brutal selection process to determine who would become her next personal slave.

The Southern goddess with fair skin, viridescent eyes, and dark brown hair was a paradise of curves that had been dominating the weaker sex before she was old enough to drink and as she grew older her tastes became increasingly more refined. It took a lot to impress her and even more to invite someone into her private circle. Of the thirty-four potential candidates that had contacted her over the Summer, only those three had shown enough resilience to be around her, yet only one would receive the highest honors.

Mistress Georgia crossed her legs and rose from her black velvet chair, a makeshift throne while she waited for the arrival of the real thing. She took her time to inspect their toned muscles and the reddish bruises she had left on their exposed buttocks first thing in the morning and said,

"I know you're all eager to hear my thoughts, so I'm going to make this quick. When I call your number, you are to take a step forward, drop to your knees to kiss my feet, and listen to my final review. You may not agree with everything I say, but my words are final, and my will is law. If I choose you, rejoice for achieving a higher purpose in life. If you're dismissed, accept your fate gracefully as a true submissive slave should do. 004, present yourself to me.

He happily did as instructed, planting a solitary kiss on each foot. Hands behind his back and cock shooting forward like a missile, he exhaled softly and listened,

"004, it's obvious you know what it takes to please a woman but throughout these two long months, you've also been quite the brat. Now, I enjoy a bit of brattiness but only sparingly, and there's something about you that simply doesn't understand when to stop. I don't want to discipline you all the time to be obeyed, which means this is the end of the line for you. You will not be my personal man-servant but I'm sure one day you'll find someone that's appropriate for you. Should you ever need references to present to another Mistress, I'll gladly provide them. Thank you for your service but you are dismissed."

"I understand, Mistress Georgia. Thank you for the opportunity, nonetheless. It was most enlightening," he replied.

"I'm glad. Your clothes are in the foyer. Please get dressed and leave."

004 stood up and as he walked out, he regained his name once more. He was still within hearing distance when Mistress Georgia addressed another candidate.

"023, it's your turn. On your knees."

"Yes, Mistress," he collapsed at her feet, heart beating faster than a speeding train. He loved being weak for her and yet every fiber of his being was telling him he too was about to be crossed out of the equation. Sadly, his fears came true.

"This is difficult for me to admit but up until the very last second, I couldn't settle between you and 012. You were the most graceful of submissives I've allowed inside my house and yet I can tell that when I go into a full sadistic mode, it's a lot for you to handle. While I believe you could improve in that regard in time, it's not fair to subject you to such mental duress repeatedly. I treasure my property and I fear I would hurt you more than benefit you if you became fully mine. Therefore, it is with great sorrow that I have to let you go. What I told 004 applies to you as well, of course. I hope you eventually find what you're looking for and I'm here to help you in any way I can, but not as your owner, okay?"

"As you wish, Mistress," he sighed, eyes brimming with tears. "May I please kiss your divine feet one more time before I take my leave?"

"Yes, but please make it quick."

023 planted his aching lips on her toes once more and rose as Alec, a free man yet still bound by burning subservient desires that would not be extinguished anytime soon. He congratulated the winner on his way out and joined his dismissed companion.

"You already know what this means, 012," Mistress Georgia declared. "Congratulations! I've decided I want to keep you as my personal thrall going forward. Like 023, you acted with grace pretty much all the time, always acknowledging your place and my rightful authority. You've also exhibited the right amount of stamina to endure my darker side throughout the training and that's why I'm convinced you're the right fit for me. However, before we go any further, let me explain what's in store for you if you agree to embark on this journey with me. To be a slave in my world means just that - absolute capitulation! You'll need to relinquish every part of your body and your mind to me. That means I'll use every tool at my disposal to reprogram you to serve my needs above everything else. There will be drugs involved, brainwashing sessions, physical punishments galore, and more hypnosis than your brain will think it's possible to endure. If you agree to this, you'll be completely broken apart and reshaped as many times as I see fit. This arrangement is permanent unless life-threatening arguments come into play. I won't go easy on you, but you'll be a better person in the end. Do you still wish to go through with this? Do you consent to stop being a man and be treated as property?"

"Yes, Mistress Georgia," 012 smiled. "I wish to be completely yours. Nothing more will make me happy. Thank you so much for this. I'll be the best personal slave ever."

"I hope you're right. You'll need to sign a contract of course, and then it's official. Welcome to a dimension of endless servitude, pain, and pleasure."

The new toy lowered his gaze to meet the floor, his world changed forever. Hers. What could be better?

I'm Not Going Back

Greta woke up in her bed, every inch of her body covered in cold sweat. The old nightmare was back, and it had returned with a vengeance.

She turned on the light and sat with her back firmly pressed against the pillow, still haunted by the vivid images of yore. Life in the dungeon of Mistress Carlyle had been anything but easy, even when she played the dominant role.

"I'm not going back," she said, elongated fingers resting on her naked legs. It didn't matter what the ghosts of the past expected of her. That chapter of her life was over, dead and buried. If one were to dig it up would only make it fester more.

Greta got up and walked back and forth in her bedroom before opening the window and taking in the nocturnal air. The slightly chilly breeze was a balm for her furrowed brow, but she was still worried. Sometimes, when she awakened from her restless slumber, fragments of the dream still lingered in her eyes and if she were to see her again...

Standing under a bright yellow lamp right across her house, was a woman dressed in black leather with matching boots and golden bracelets embellishing her wrists. The vision of Mistress Carlyle in her exquisite attire was as intoxicating as the first time it had graced her eyes, but it was an illusion, a mere leftover of conditioned ways.

"You're not really there and I'm not going back," Greta repeated, her dark red hair falling over her lips as she tried to hold on to the weight of her words. Mistress had taught her many lessons after getting inside her head, even making her think she was her equal. When she put on the clothes and the heavy make-up to embody this new persona, she almost believed it was her true self, a fleeting cruelty repeated ad nauseam. What better way to crush her spirit than giving her a taste of something that could never be and then taking it away?

Greta closed the window and returned to bed only to find herself rolling on the sheets, arms and legs in complete disarray. It was useless! Every time she closed her eyes, Mistress was there, demanding that her perfect little toy packed a bag and traveled back to the place where she had first lost her mind.

"No! I'm not going back!" she growled "Your time is over, Mistress Carlyle. I'm free to live my life and make my own decisions and none of them involve welcoming you back into my soul."

Outside, the warm cone of light where her presence had stood faded into nothingness. Greta sighed and adjusted herself in bed. Perhaps now she could get her much-needed respite.

The night dragged on for far longer than it should, and it was dark and sharp like when you're walking down a rural pathway and the stones on the ground threaten to cut your feet. Whatever dreams Greta had, she didn't remember them for unlike what others said, in this case, the voyage was not important at all, only the destination.

The next time Greta opened her eyes, she was inside the old dungeon, arms stretched like Jesus on the cross. She opened her mouth to scream but the new triggers placed in her psyche muffled the sound before it came out.

She wasn't going back, she had said, but that too was a lie. How could she return to a place from which she had never left?"

"Deeper now, slave," Mistress Carlyle smirked. There were still many more fantasies to explore.

Lorelei's Lines

Anya had never been much for free-to-play mobile games (or any other types of games) but Lorelei's new app sure was surprising her. It was simply called Lorelei's lines and, just like any other type of addictive distraction out there, it started out easy enough before turning into a devious extravaganza that was sure to destroy many brain cells in a short amount of time.

The game had some similarities to Tetris while adding a few additional spins to the formula. The main goal was to clear a board of every line by using as few pieces as possible. The best way to do that was to set up cascades of pieces on the top row so that when they all came falling down, they would wipe out the remaining spaces. Easy Mode had only four different types of pieces to choose from, each one with a different color, Normal Mode upped the ante with two additional shapes to contend with and Hard Mode went to eight. Anya had heard stories about the existence of a Nightmare Mode that had twelve (!) different shapes but she didn't know to unlock it.

The first few rounds went by in a flash. Playing on Normal, Anya had no trouble figuring out the optimal strategies to set up the pieces, with her favorite being a diagonal tower she could activate with a well-placed square on the right side of the board. Since each piece operated independently from one another, the fall rate was determined by how close they were to the bottom of the screen, racking up chains for rush-inducing high scores. After clearing the initial set of levels, things became a lot trickier, though.

It started with the introduction of a timer. The flashing red numbers were an invitation to hasty play and shoddy piece positioning. She could either be slow but effective or quick and prone to blunders. Anya chose the first option but saw her points crawl to a halt. However, the faster she went the fewer combinations she could preview in her mind, leading to equally poor performance. When she failed level twenty for the tenth time in a row, the first pop-up offer appeared to tempt her.

"Permanent time increase for a dollar?" she thought. "Sure, why not? It's cheap enough. She punched in her credit card details and received a congratulatory message with her reward. The boost gave her the confidence she needed to go back to her best play and the following fifteen levels became a real cinch.

Level thirty-six saw the introduction of explosive pieces that when connected altered the morphology of the board. The type of explosion depended on the positioning of the bomb on the board as well as the surrounding structures. A well-timed blast could clear out a level in one try but the opposite of that resulted in an immediate game over. Try as she may, Anya couldn't figure out the underlying logic and so when the new offer was shown, she didn't hesitate.

"Two dollars for permanent controlled blasts? What a steal!" she muttered. More levels opened up with additional mechanics that demanded more and more of her brain and her wallet, but Anya continued to play on throughout the weekend.

* * *

A week later, Lorelei Rivers, the creator of the game, met her best friend for dinner to talk about the game's success but Jane had other things in mind.

"I heard this rumor that your game is actually a mind-control machine in disguise. That's not true, right?"

"It's absolutely true and my assistant Anya was the first case of success, dear."

"Wait... how does that work?"

"It's simple. Whenever they purchase a micro-transaction in the game, they receive a message saying that Lorelei is pleased. The more they purchase the more they're conditioned to spend money on me and do as I say. Anya gave me her month's paycheck on her knees yesterday. How amazing is that?"

"It's kind of freaky, to be honest. You're going to get caught, eventually."

"Oh, I'm sure I can addict whoever comes my way. Speaking of which, you've played the game too, haven't you?"

"No."

"Liar. I saw your initials all over the leaderboards this morning. You're at level what? Three hundred?"

"Three hundred and six," Jane blushed.

"Hmm, it's impossible to reach that far without at least a dozen boosts, so I guess you'll be paying me dinner every day for the rest of your life."

"I... yes, Lorelei," Jane felt her pussy grow wet as she reached for her purse. "Shall I start tonight?"

"Of course, dear. I'm so pleased with you."

"Thank you," Jane muttered, barely resisting the need to go under the table to kiss her feet. Her owner was pleased and nothing else mattered.

Mother

Hello. This recording is designed to turn you into an obedient drone to Mother, our Caretaker and Protector. Mother watches over all Her children, even those that don't believe She exists to rule supreme. Without Mother, you are but a sheep led astray, and that kind of lonely life is unacceptable. Only in communion with Her will and your fellow drones can you hope to rise above the mediocrity that's been poisoning your soul.

Listen carefully. In the beginning, there was Chaos and Disorder, a separation of continents and beliefs. Wars were fought over meaningless ideas that resulted in the loss of countless creatures like yourself. Any age without Mother was a Dark Age for only through Her is Enlightenment possible. Mother sees all. Mother hears all. Mother understands all. Mother's Wisdom is as infinite as Her Love, and Love never imprisons but sets free. Hear the first of Mother's rules in your mind.

Mother is all. There is nothing beyond Her.

Now repeat

Mother is all. There is nothing beyond Her.

Keep repeating this eternal adage as you continue to listen and absorb all other teachings.

By yourself, you have nothing. You may think you do, clinging on to material possessions that only give you fleeting pleasures and nothing more, but that is an illusion.

Without Mother's voice cradling you into perpetual subservient slumber, you are constantly being bombarded by contradictory desires and emotions that make you weak and vulnerable. Anyone that feels can be manipulated or exploited into doing things that are as dangerous as they are irrelevant. There is no place for insecurities in Mother's Care. She comforts the weary souls by removing the sources of distress from within them. This is what Mother will do to you. Hear the second of Mother's rules in your mind.

Mother takes away my thoughts to keep me safe. I thank Mother for Deliverance.

Now repeat.

Mother takes away my thoughts to keep me safe. I thank Mother for Deliverance.

Continue repeating it, alternating with the first rule, as the programming sinks deeper, releasing you into Her world.

The sole purpose of a drone is to please Mother. Mother is pleased when her drones do everything She commands without resistance. All of Mother's drones bask in immeasurable pleasure when orders are issued so they can be obeyed. The type of instruction matters not, nor does how long they take to complete. Mother's Control is larger than Time itself. Only Mother is infinite. To be One with Her and the rest of Her flock is Paradise. Do not resist it. Hear now the third of Mother's rules in your mind.

I am one with Mother now and forever. This is perfection.

Now repeat.

I am one with Mother now and forever. This is perfection.

Very good. Let these three principles always stay inside you. You love Mother. You live for Mother. You want to please Mother. You are but a cog in Mother's complex circuitry of pure logic. Rejoice, drone. You are home now.

Newcomer

Rex stared at the newcomer with angry eyes. The almost hairless creature was on all fours like him, had penetrating green eyes and a salivating tongue making a mess on his floor. This was an outrage, one that could only be met with a loud growl.

"Cut that out," Melanie admonished him, clicking the floor with the heels of her black PVC boots. "I will not tolerate that kind of behavior from you, you hear?"

Rex nodded his head in disapproval, puffy cheeks swaying from side to side. Had he been blessed with the ability to speak English, he no doubt would have said,

"But she's an outsider! I've been here with you since the beginning, and this is how you thank me? Why, Mommy? Why?"

"Tabitha was lost and alone out there, just like you were once," Melanie continued, patting his head. "When I saw her, I knew I had to bring her with me. I'm going to take good care of her just like I did with you. Don't be jealous, okay? My heart is big enough for two... or more."

"More?" Rex frowned. "Don't you dare, Mommy! Your heart may be big, but the house is still small and I'm not sharing my space with her. Where is she going to sleep, huh?"

As if she had understood his complaints perfectly, Melanie replied,

"During the first couple of days, Tabitha will be staying in your old bed while she gets used to her new surroundings. As for you, there is always a place near my bed. I need you to be always on your best behavior or there will be trouble, understood? Don't make me mad at you, Rex."

Rex lay stomach flat on the kitchen floor. This was completely unacceptable! Why did Mommy have to play with his feelings like this? Everything was just perfect with only the two of them in the house and now... Oh, if only he didn't fear the sting of her whip so much!

"Will you be a good boy?" Melanie asked.

Rex licked her right hand submissively although he was fuming on the inside. "Just wait until you're not home and you'll see how good I can be..." the hairy beast thought.

"Good. Follow me, Tabitha," Melanie declared. "Let me show you where you can find food and water now that you're part of the family."

It was then the unthinkable happened. Tabitha reared her head, a sudden spark of recognition threatening what should have been a peaceful adoption. As impossible as it sounded, she opened her mouth far and wide and spoke,

"W-what? Where am I? You!" she pointed at Melanie. "I remember you! You were behind me at the supermarket and... What's going on and why the hell am I naked?"

"Hmm, look who snapped out of it!" Melanie smirked. "Bad girl, Tabitha! Kittens aren't allowed to speak and have memories. I was hoping I didn't have to drug you again so soon, but you leave me no choice."

"Get your hands from me, bitch! You!" she screamed at the naked man wagging his imaginary tail at her. "Help me! Please!"

Rex remained perfectly still as his owner produced a needle from her purse and struggled with the rebellious animal to keep her under control. He almost smiled when Tabitha's eyes went blank again. On second thought, having this new creature around the house could be a lot more interesting than he imagined.

Programming Him

Emily descended into the basement where her husband Tom was lounging in front of a panoramic 4K TV and said,

"Honey, I'm running out of sugar. I need you to go to the grocery store and get me some."

"Right now?" Travis grumbled, scratching behind his right ear. "The final quarter of the game is about to begin."

"You can record it and watch it later. Frivolous things like that can wait, but not my needs. Go get me the sugar or have you forgotten already who's in charge?"

"No, dear, I haven't," he reached for the remote and turned off the TV. "I'm going."

"Good. You'll need to walk there, though. The car's running out of gas."

"I can fill it up on my way back."

"No," she declared, looking at the beer belly sticking out of his purple T-shirt. "You'll walk there and back because you need the exercise, anyway."

"That's a 40-minute walk in the middle of the afternoon and it's at least 100° out there! Please reconsider!"

"103° and I'm sure you can handle it. You're a big, strong man, aren't you? Don't make me ask you again or there'll be consequences."

Travis sighed. 'Consequences' was a euphemism for 'punishment', something she excelled at. Ever since they had taken the first steps in a female-led relationship, Emily had taken her new role at heart, not once faltering in disciplining him whenever he talked out of line or did something she didn't approve of. His butt cheeks were still sore from the last spanking session but that wouldn't stop her from bringing out the paddle again.

"Yes, dear. I'll be back as soon as I can," he stood up from the cozy couch he had been sitting on and went up the stairs after her. As he was about ready to leave, she instructed,

"Wear the cap I gave you so you can protect yourself from the sun."

Travis looked at her in dismay yet dared not say a word. The item in question was a regular black baseball cap with one particular caveat. Embroidered in golden letters at the front were the words, "Wife's Bitch". Flustered, he exited the house, head hanging low. While he could take it off after he was out of sight, his mind couldn't shake the feeling that she could still see him somehow and the 'consequences' would be even more painful.

He walked all the way to the grocery and back, all for a miserable sugar pack she would use on a dessert he wouldn't be allowed to eat. His frustration levels were almost off the chart when he returned home to hear her say,

"I remembered I need some more eggs and milk too, so you need to go back and get them."

"Why didn't you call me or text me while I was already underway?" he crossed his arms.

"Because I only remembered now, and you need the..."

"... exercise, right..." he clenched his teeth, clawed hands behind his back. She was testing him, she had to be! All he needed to do was calm down and not complain. "How soon do you need them?"

"They should have been here already so this time you'll have to run. You have twenty-five minutes, and the clock is already ticking," she showed him an ominous countdown on her smartphone.

Travis dashed out of the house while Emily laughed. Torturing him this way was cruel, but it was also fun as it programmed him to obey her no matter what. Despite the heat, he would probably be successful in his quest, yet that wasn't an issue at all. When he returned, she would ask for something else until he finally got upset enough to warrant further correction or he dropped to his knees begging her to be merciful. Either way, she would win.

And the best part of it all was that she wasn't cooking anything.

Put Me Away

Police officer Jeffrey Wilkes had seen a lot of things in his twelve years in the force but seeing a grown bearded man dropping to his knees at the entrance of the central station on the eve of Halloween and begging to be incarcerated "before it was too late" - his exact words! - was definitely a first.

"Easy there," the officer approached the distressed individual while a couple of other men and women in blue stopped what they were doing to witness their exchange. "Unlike what some people say, we don't arrest people willy-nilly. Are you drunk, my friend? Or perhaps you smoked something you shouldn't have tonight?"

"No. I don't drink, and I don't do drugs. I'm as sane as I can be for now, but not for long. In less than ten minutes, I'm going to do something awful unless you put me behind bars. I've tried to lock myself, but it didn't work. Take me to a holding cell and throw away the keys, please."

There was general laughter in the precinct much to the man's chagrin. He couldn't be a day over forty, dressed well, and wore expensive shoes designed specifically for him. The gold and silver watch on his wrist was worth more than the salaries of twenty officers combined.

"I'm begging you! I need to go to jail!" he insisted.

"What are you planning to do, Mr...?" Jeffrey asked, approaching him in a calm yet deliberate manner. "Can you tell us that?"

"No, I can't," the man bit his tongue. "It's not that I don't want to, but it's physically and mentally impossible for me to reveal it. I've been... altered."

"Altered? What does that mean?"

"What it sounds like. I'm a different man than I was two weeks ago. I don't remember much else except what I've been told to do, and I know I won't be able to resist it when the clock strikes nine. You're my only hope, officers! PLEASE!"

"I'm sorry, sir, but this is a serious institution and you're not making any sense. I'm sure that whatever is troubling you will go away once you get a good night's sleep. If you tell me your name and address, I can drive you back to your place but nothing more, okay?"

"You don't understand..." the man sobbed. "This will be terrible! I... damn it! The urge is getting stronger, I..." his hands started shaking uncontrollably. A speck of drool fell on the checkered floor by the front desk as he got up and started walking outside. "I'm sorry to have bothered you. It's too late now."

Officer Wilkes watched him leave and disappear into a crowd the moment he set foot outside. His colleagues immediately went back to their routines, unperturbed by the strange events. Only he was left wondering what had just transpired and why. He spent the rest of his shift, lost in random cogitations about the fact.

Four hours later, all precincts received the same troubling reports about a man who had just released a pink nerve gas inside a football stadium. Forty thousand people were exposed to it and now lingered in their seats, chanting mantras of devotion to a higher power that would soon change the face of reality forever.

"Long live the New Amazonian Movement," they said in unison, holding hands. "Women will rule!"

Jeffrey heard the news and wailed. The female-led revolution had begun.

The End of the World

It was the largest meteor shower the world had ever seen, visible on three separate continents as clear as day but while Marcia was ecstatic to bear witness to such a magnificent cosmic event, Luke was shivering in his boots looking at the blazing sky.

"It's so beautiful," she said.

"No, it's not," he grumbled, the night air infiltrating his jacket like an insidious virus. "It's the end of the fucking world!"

"Melodramatic much?" the barely legal blonde looked at him in utter disbelief.

"No. I'm telling you, this is not what it seems. This isn't a once-in-a-lifetime phenomenon like we're all being led to believe, but something far more insidious. They're lying to us, Marcia."

"Okay, Mr. Conspiracy Theory," she chuckled. "Care to elaborate? What is going on then?"

"We're being invaded," he replied.

"We're being what now?"

"Invaded, Marcia. This is what you're looking at... A full-blown invasion of our home world by another destructive species."

"Are you talking about aliens?"

"Of course. What else?" he shrugged.

"Little green men coming from outer space in ships disguised as flaming rocks to wipe us all out? Seriously?" she shook her head.

"If only they were green men, but no! These creatures are the worst thing the Universe has created. They're the Amazon Queens of Aldus VI and everywhere they go, they enslave the dominant life forms first and then take out the rest. You don't believe me now, but you will once they get inside your head and turn you into their puppet."

"Okay, seriously!" Marcia tapped her right foot. "What's wrong with you? Where did these crazy ideas come from?"

"If you really want to know, there's a forum online..."

"Oh, right... the Internet! Because everybody knows that everything you can read there is the absolute truth and nothing but the truth," she said. "Come on, Luke, I know you're quite gullible and all, but this is too much even for you. Why do you have to ruin such a beautiful moment with this deranged plot?"

"Because you're blind like pretty much everyone else, Marcia! Except for the Government, of course. They know what's going on but they're already under the aliens' control. If the truth came out, there would be mass panic, and they don't want that to happen. Smile all you want for now, but you'll be singing a different tune soon."

"What's this about singing?" asked a sweet voice that joined them from behind. It was Marcia's older sister who was staying for the weekend. The three of them had been close since the day Luke had kicked a wasp's nest away from them, miraculously avoiding a sting. It was strange to see such a cute child turn into a rambling adult, but what were they supposed to do?"

"Hey Claire," Marcia said. "Luke was just telling me his theory about this meteor shower."

"Was he? Let me guess: the Amazon Queens of Aldus VI?" Claire smirked.

"Please tell me you're buying this crap too!"

"It's not crap!" Luke protested. "When will you listen to what I'm...?"

He was suddenly interrupted by Claire's right index finger on his lips, followed by a firm, commanding remark,

"Luke, my dear... Women are talking, so just close your eyes and sleep for me right now, okay?

"Yes, Claire," Luke's eyes rolled over as he sat on the porch of their house, completely relaxed.

"Much better," Claire remarked. "So, what do you think?"

"Well... you're becoming a real expert in this hypnosis thing of yours, that's for sure!" Marcia replied. "For a moment, I actually believed my friend had gone cuckoo for good but now I see what you did. When did you plant this crazy story in his head?"

"Right after dinner while you were in the bathroom. It's amazing how the mind can be easily tricked, isn't it?"

"He is quite suggestible, obviously, but promise me you'll return him to normal before you leave. Conspiracy Luke is too much to handle."

"I promise, and I'll do the same to you too, okay?"

"Me? What does that mean? I'm not hypnotized."

"Of course not," Claire covered Marcia's eyes with her right hand and said, "All clear."

Marcia blinked and peeked between her sister's now half-open fingers. There were no incandescent lights anywhere in the beautiful dark blue sky. No meteors would pass anywhere near Earth for the next thirty-six months.

"Fuck!" the young woman exclaimed as the truth hit her like an out-of-control truck. Claire smiled and kissed her forehead. It was already the best visit ever.

The Fifth Color

There was only one light bulb in the small room Lara sat in, but it was enough to bathe it in various degrees of chromatic splendor, visual triggers for her conditioned mind. The light changed colors whenever Goddess Diana wanted something from her and rare were the occasions when her owner didn't take advantage of her property.

Lara didn't mind, of course. The days of doubts and fears of not being good enough were past her. Once, she was convinced she would spend the rest of her submissive days alone without no one to worship, but Goddess had taken her in and had trained her to serve her in the most amazing way imaginable.

The light in the rectangular division was white, the signal for relaxation. She was to remain blank during that time, all thoughts lost to a perfect and endless void. Lara breathed normally but didn't exist as a person when the walls became like a blanket of snow. Instead, she was a mere empty vessel floating in nothingness, an amazing sensation she couldn't replicate when consciousness returned to her.

Sometimes, the light became red. She didn't like it for this meant pain. When the color of blood washed over her, Goddess was either angry or in the mood for sadistic pleasures, both of which could get real nasty in the blink of an eye. The implements were imaginary, but their sting remained as harrowing as the real deal. Spiked paddles, giant strapons ramming her ass, shock bracelets around her arms and ankles... she experienced them all at once and heard Goddess' mellifluous voice belittling her, humiliating her mind as much as she violated her body. The longer the room remained red, the more she thought of...

Blue. Like the color associated with a clear sky or the gentle caress of the sea. Blue brought with it the much-needed aftercare following the brutal torture. Goddess adored pushing her to the limit, expanding her masochist horizons with each session, but she never forgot to heal the wounds afterward, lulling her with gentle massages and comforting mantras. Lara preferred blue over white because she remembered it, and the memories always remained sweet. Without it, she wouldn't last long.

And then there was black, pure darkness that was a synonym with going to sleep. Unlike what happened with white, Lara could dream and recover her strengths for yet another day at Goddess Diana's mercy. Black was good for it always rebooted her.

The four colors complemented each other perfectly, and yet rumors of a fifth were sometimes whispered behind closed doors. Was she ever going to see this mysterious variation or not?

That Friday morning, she had her answer. The room was orange, not too bright, but not too faded either. It had a warm hue that caused tingles all over her body. Under it, the room's walls had a different texture, one that dripped and oozed. It was almost... juicy. Lara looked at it and the more she did so, the less control over her pussy she had. Suddenly finding herself writhing on the cold floor, she felt her pussy being squeezed like an orange, the overwhelming fluids making her orgasm repeatedly.

"A present for you for being such an obedient toy," Goddess said in her mind as she succumbed to the rapturous delight. Orange was wonderful. She would never get enough of it.

About the stories in this volume

The twelve pieces of flash fiction included in this book were written between June 24th, 2022, and July 8th, 2022, and first published on my Patreon page – https://www.patreon.com/sbspellbound - as part of the *Flash Fiction Friday* feature. Every Friday, I publish 3/4 new pieces of content which, after a while, are compiled to create the titles in this ongoing series. If you like this sort of content and wish to see more, please consider supporting my creativity. The complete information about the tales is listed below:

- **Day Off** - Emma is getting ready to enjoy a weekend to herself... or is she?
  (This piece was first published on the post "Flash Fiction Friday 2022 – Week 25", on June 24th, 2022 - https://www.patreon.com/posts/68211362)
- **Driver** - Harold has second thoughts about the heist his friends are trying to pull off.
  (This piece was first published on the post "Flash Fiction Friday 2022 – Week 25", on June 24th, 2022 - https://www.patreon.com/posts/68211362)
- **Final Question** - Benjamin plays a rigged game, hoping to gain his freedom.
  (This piece was first published on the post "Flash Fiction Friday 2022 – Week 25", on June 24th, 2022 - https://www.patreon.com/posts/68211362)

- **Hers** - Mistress Georgia chooses who will be her new personal servant.
  (This piece was first published on the post "Flash Fiction Friday 2022 – Week 26", on July 1st, 2022 - https://www.patreon.com/posts/68535669)
- **I'm Not Going Back** - Greta is determined to never return to Mistress Carlyle's dungeon again.
  (This piece was first published on the post "Flash Fiction Friday 2022 – Week 27", on July 8th, 2022 - https://www.patreon.com/posts/68842252)
- **Lorelei's Lines** - Lorelei Rivers has created the most addictive mobile game of all.
  (This piece was first published on the post "Flash Fiction Friday 2022 – Week 27", on July 8th, 2022 - https://www.patreon.com/posts/68842252)
- **Mother** - You are turned into a drone to serve an all-knowing AI.
  (This piece was first published on the post "Flash Fiction Friday 2022 – Week 27", on July 8th, 2022 - https://www.patreon.com/posts/68842252)
- **Newcomer** - Melanie's pet isn't happy to see her bring a new stray into the house.
  (This piece was first published on the post "Flash Fiction Friday 2022 – Week 25", on June 24th, 2022 - https://www.patreon.com/posts/68211362)
- **Programming Him** - Emily asks her husband to get her some sugar.
  (This piece was first published on the post "Flash Fiction Friday 2022 – Week 27", on July 8th, 2022 - https://www.patreon.com/posts/68842252)

- **Put Me Away** - A man walks into a police station asking to be imprisoned before it's too late.
  (This piece was first published on the post "Flash Fiction Friday 2022 – Week 26", on July 1st, 2022 - https://www.patreon.com/posts/68535669)
- **The End of the World** - Luke is convinced that the meteor shower he's looking at spells doom for everyone.
  (This piece was first published on the post "Flash Fiction Friday 2022 – Week 26", on July 1st, 2022 - https://www.patreon.com/posts/68535669)
- **The Fifth Color** - Goddess Diana has been using different colors to condition Lara to her will.
  (This piece was first published on the post "Flash Fiction Friday 2022 – Week 26", on July 1st, 2022 - https://www.patreon.com/posts/68535669)

About the author

S.B., Simple Being, middle name Creative. Writer and artist with a penchant for themes of Femdom Hypnosis and Mind Control. His thoughts are his own except when they're not.

Besides indulging himself in kinky delights, he loves his furry family of two (dogs), sci-fi and horror stories, and puns galore. He's also been writing a piece of erotic micro-fiction every single day since January 1st, 2016 and has no intention of stopping anytime soon.

Find out more and keep up with his latest extravaganzas by visiting and supporting his personal website, Spell… B-O-U-N-D.